The Superpov
Game_

by Steve Cole
Illustrated by Bill Ledger

OXFORD
UNIVERSITY PRESS

In this story ...

Ben
(Sprint)

Ben is super fast! He can run faster than a racing car. Once, he ran five times round the school grounds in under ten seconds.

Evan
(Flex)

Nisha
(Nimbus)

Mr Trainer
(teacher)

Chapter 1:
Tough team training

"Come on, team!" Sprint shouted to the other Hero Academy pupils as he ran around the track. "This is our last chance to practise."

The heroes were preparing for the Superpower Games, which were starting that afternoon.

THE SUPERPOWER GAMES

The Superpower Games is the most exciting and important superhero sports competition in the world! Young superheroes compete against each other in a series of thrilling contests, held over two days. The winner of each contest receives a medal.

At the end of the two days, the school with the most medals receives the Superpower Games Cup.

Events include:
- speed test race
- dodgeball
- hover-kart racing
- super-strength trials

"I could keep this up all day," Flex said, playing dodgeball with a couple of practice robots. His arms and legs were stretched so thin that they looked like strands of spaghetti. "The team from Superpower School will never beat us."

"Too right!" shouted Nimbus from her speeding hover-kart. She was using wind-power to blow herself faster around the track. "They'll be eating our dust!" she shouted, as she sped past Sprint.

"Ugh!" said Sprint. "Our dust tastes horrible. They're welcome to it!"

Sprint began to wheeze, so he stopped running. "I need my inhaler."

Flex brought over Sprint's bag and handed him his inhaler. "Take it easy for a minute, Sprint," he said. "Your job as team captain is to look after *everyone*, including yourself."

"Sorry, Sprint," said Nimbus, stopping beside him.

"That's ... all ... right," said Sprint. He took a puff of his inhaler, waited a few moments, then put the inhaler back in his bag. As he did so, Sprint heard a faint whirring sound in the sky. He looked up. "You know ... that funny-shaped cloud has been there all morning," he said. "It's stayed in exactly the same place."

Nimbus frowned. "That's odd. Clouds normally blow away … like this!" She whipped up a gust of wind and hurled it at the cloud, but the cloud didn't move.

Scowling, Nimbus blew up a real gale. This time, the cloud began to break apart in big fluffy clumps.

Nimbus gasped. "That's not a real cloud at all!" she exclaimed.

Behind the fake cloud was a video camera hovering in the air.

"That's a heli-cam," Flex said.

"I don't believe it!" Sprint gasped. "Someone's spying on us!"

Chapter 2:
I spy trouble

The heli-cam made a loud *BEEP!* and quickly zoomed away.

"Whoever sent that heli-cam knows we've seen it," Flex said. "It must be heading back to where it came from."

"I'll follow it," Sprint said.

"Are you sure you're all right to do that?"
Nimbus asked, concerned.

Sprint nodded. "I feel
much better now,"
he said.

Sprint raced across the academy grounds.
He slipped through an ordinary-looking doorway
that was used as the secret entrance to Hero
Academy, and into the city streets.

The heli-cam was so far away, it looked like a dot in the sky. Sprint was determined to catch up, though! He dashed across the city, zigzagging around lamp-posts and rubbish bins so fast that nobody saw him.

Sprint stopped when he saw the heli-cam drop down from the sky. It headed towards the door of a second-hand bookshop. Sprint knew that this was the entrance to Superpower School.

"So," Sprint thought crossly. *"That's* who's been spying on us!"

The shop door opened, and the heli-cam vanished inside.

Sprint raced back to Hero Academy and told the other heroes what he'd seen.

"I can't believe they've been watching us train!" Nimbus said with a groan.

"Now they'll know our strengths and weaknesses," said Sprint. "They'll know what to expect, and they'll be able to match us."

"Or beat us," added Flex crossly. "There are only three hours until the Superpower Games, and we don't know a thing about their team … We should tell Mr Trainer."

"But he'll cancel the Games if he finds out they've cheated," Sprint replied. "We can still win."

"How?" asked Nimbus.

Sprint grinned. "By being ourselves – only in a way they don't expect …"

Later that day, as the start of the Games drew near, Sprint stood in the changing rooms and watched the excited crowd fill the stadium. He felt nerves buzzing in his belly. Would his plan work?

The Superpower School bus arrived, and the young athletes clambered off, led by their PE teacher, Miss Gatsby. She introduced Sprint to her team captain, a boy called Blur.

After Miss Gatsby had left to discuss the rules with Mr Trainer, Blur held up the video camera that he'd been using to spy on them. He smirked at Sprint, Flex and Nimbus. "You know," he said, "I'm sure I've seen you all somewhere before ..."

"Unfortunately for you, it won't make any difference to the Games," said Sprint.

Blur stopped smirking. "What do you mean?"

As a bell rang to call the athletes to their starting places, Nimbus smiled at Blur. "You'll see!"

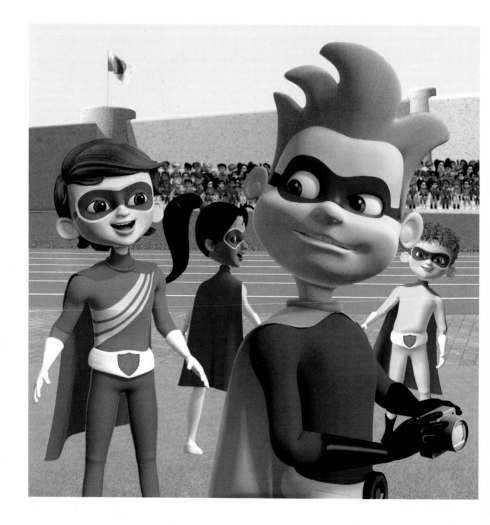

Chapter 3:
The games begin!

"Remember our plan," Sprint told his team. "I know we're taking a risk, but we can do this!"

Nimbus and Flex nodded with nervous smiles.

"Good luck, all!" said Mr Trainer.

"The first event is the speed test race," Miss Gatsby announced.

Blur strode over. "My power is super-speed too. I can go so fast that my legs are a blur. So, Sprint, I'm up against you."

"Actually, I'm not in that race," said Sprint. "Nimbus is."

"What?" Blur cried.

"You heard!" Nimbus said with a grin.

Blur's mouth dropped open.

Nimbus conjured up a mini-tornado. It picked
her up and whizzed her along the track really
fast. Blur just couldn't keep up!

Nimbus flew across the finishing line.

"We have a winner!" Miss Gatsby declared.

"That's not fair!" Blur wailed. "Sprint was meant to run that race."

Mr Trainer replied, "The rules clearly state that schools can enter whoever they choose into each event."

Miss Gatsby frowned at Blur. "How did you know that Sprint was meant to take part in that event?"

Blur blushed. "Er …"

Mr Trainer said, "Let's move on to the next event."

Sprint took part in the dodgeball event instead of Flex. With his super-speed, he could easily dodge his opponent's power balls, and hurl the balls back just as fast.

"Sprint is the champion!" said Mr Trainer at the end.

Flex took Nimbus's place in the hover-karting. He stretched his super-flexible body like a sail on a ship so he could go even faster.

"That was a good use of your powers," said Mr Trainer. "First place to Flex!"

For the rest of the afternoon, the other heroes from Hero Academy continued to win their events.

Finally, Miss Gatsby announced, "That was the last event. The school who won the most medals today is … Hero Academy!"

"Yes!" Sprint punched the air while Flex and Nimbus high-fived.

"It's not fair!" Blur said. He threw his camera on the ground. "We were going to beat you ... until you put different athletes in for every event."

"Blur!" Miss Gatsby exclaimed. "How would you know that Hero Academy swapped their athletes?"

Blur froze. "Er ... lucky guess?" he said feebly.

Miss Gatsby picked up the camera and pressed the play button. She gasped. "You were spying on Hero Academy! I will not have cheats representing our school." She switched off the camera. "Blur, you are disqualified from competing tomorrow!"

As Blur stormed off, Sprint and his friends went up to receive their medals. The crowd cheered and clapped.

"Well done, everyone," Sprint said to his team.

"Congratulations," added Miss Gatsby.

Mr Trainer nodded proudly. "You've all earned your medals today ... each one of you in your own unique way!"